Poems About Pigeons & Other Incidental Things

A debut collection of Anecdote and Reflection

By Pam Ski

Poems About Pigeons & Other Incidental Things

ISBN: 9798863753775
© Pam Szadowski, October, 2023

E-mail: poemsbypamski@gmail.com

Published independently by Robin Barratt
www.RobinBarratt.co.uk

About The Author

A child of the '60s, Pam grew up on The Wirral, Merseyside, in North West England, and learnt to read from rhyming stories in comics. She has always loved the rhythm and intensity of poetry, but has only recently begun to write regularly.

Several of her poems have appeared in print in local and national newspapers, and a couple of her poems have been included in collections such as the Poetry for Mental Health book series and shortlisted in Ó Bhéal Cork Poetry Society's annual competition.

In March 2023 Pam won the monthly Dreading Slam poetry competition in Reading, the area where she now lives.

E: poemsbypamski@gmail.com

Acknowledgements

Thank you to my children Kate, Zak and Jed and my granddaughters Maya and Eve who have inspired me to write. And thanks to wider family and friends for their encouragement to publish, with a special mention to: Tasha Bryant, Claudia Kirkpatrick, Deborah Ellert, Carole Samuda and Sharon and Richard Norton.

In loving memory of my husband
Trevor, 1957 - 2021, and my son
Josh, 1978 - 2007.

Contents

Part 1: Life As We Know It

Part 2: The Time of My Life

Part 3: Pure Daftness

Part 4: Stuff To Think About

Part 5: Me, Myself & I

Part 1:

Life As We Know It

An Irrational Hatred

Relatively harmless
grey-feathered things ...
We call them "vermin"
Or "Rats with wings."

Maybe ... it's familiarity that
breeds contempt ... or the
risk of droppings ... making
us ... mucky and unkempt.

To be fair ... there is a
crazy-amount of poo, but
unless you inhale or ingest it,
it probably won't harm you.

They rarely dive-bomb us
as we walk along the street,
Seem to enjoy fluttering and
scuttering around our feet.

So I sometimes wonder, though
Beauty's in the eye of the beholder ...
Would we be nicer to pigeons,
If their plumage was ... bolder?

Trigger Happy

Someone sends you a text
With some devastating news,
'n' you're trying to come up with
the exact-right words to choose.

As you finish tapping and
your finger extends to "send",
... what goes whizzing off is a
cheery thumbs-up to your friend!

Mermaids

Hacking through the rainforest,
How mighty Amazon roars,
As it swirls past us minions
On a mission of lost cause.

Combing the beaches of eBay,
For treasures of every kind,
Turning over loose pebbles
For our missing piece of mind.

Afloat on Insta's life raft,
Tossing out quips and gripes!
Lots of jolly followers …
We're counting on their likes!

Foraging Google's forests,
Trekking across the aps,
Knights on a quest for mermaids,
Or just ourselves perhaps.

Space Thief

Clutter is the thief of space!
It sidles through our front door!
It creeps up on us ... bit by bit
'Til our home can't take any more.

Paperwork is a sneaky fiend!
Each sliver ... so ultra-thin!
But those piles turn into teetering-
towers that overpower the bin!

Wiring winds us up in knots,
We're terrified to throw it away ...
Reams 'n' reams of random leads,
We might just need some day!

Photos sabotage our senses,
It's difficult to discard any!
Few hard copies now ... mostly digital,
But we already have so many!

Holiday souvenirs reel us in,
The sun shines bright on the tat!
But the novelty soon wears off,
Why on earth did we buy that?

Kitchen paraphernalia
Spreads like a contagion,
From fondues to spiralizers:
A gadget for every occasion!

All that should be in the loft
Are suitcases for foreign travels,
And ... Christmas decorations
But that plan soon unravels!

We're historic hunter-gatherers:
Hard-wired to ... accumulate,
We'd better ... genetically modify
Ourselves ... before it is too late!

Celebrity

Paparazzi
capture
slips and spills,

Schadenfreude
of cheap thrills!

Revelling in
the dishevelled
state of stars

If they depart,
it's all
hand-on-mouth
and
heart-on-sleeve
compassion …

Humanity is
Back in Fashion.

Seaside Cavalcade

Sound the fanfare of summer:
A ninety-nine-cornet parade!
Come in Kias ... Come in Mercs!
Join our seaside cavalcade!

Roll-up ... Roll-up the tinfoil sea!
Roll-out ... the golden strand
The beach-playground is open,
But ... we're running out of sand!

Quick, unfurl that tartan blanket!
Let's stake some sort of claim!
Grab our own secluded patch!
Everyone else is doing the same!

A stripy windbreak ... even better!
As effective as the Berlin Wall!
Cheek-by-jowl at the British seaside ...
We're having an absolute ball!

One Of Those things

As mythical as unicorns,
roaming ancient plains.

As fantastical as dragons,
with breath full of flames.

As imaginary as mermaids
in crystal-clear oceans.

Or broom-riding witches
with iridescent potions.

As fanciful as fairies with
gossamer-spun wings.

Or seeing your GP in person ...
What a truly amazing thing!

Britishness

Summer fetes:
As quintessentially British,
As bright and breezy bunting!
But some of us are hooked on
boot-sales 'n' treasure-hunting!

Cricket teas:
As quintessentially British,
As a clash like ... Yorks v Surrey!
But some of us would rather head
off to the Indian for a curry.

Queuing:
As quintessentially British,
As sipping tea from china-cups,
But these days ...we're standing
in line for mugs of Starbucks' stuff.

TV soaps:
As quintessentially British,
As Corrie's cobbled streets ...
But some prefer to watch BGT
with all its daft 'n' daring feats!

John Lewis:
As quintessentially British,
As "Are You Being Served",
But Primark is a whole lot
less-punishing on the purse!

So what makes
Us quintessentially British...
When none of us are the same?
Some: clutching brollies ...
Others: sprinting in the rain ...

Probably less about the choices,
Than the right to take our pick ...
And how we try ... to be un-bothered
about the boxes ... other people tick.

Part 2:

The Time of My Life

Are We Nearly There Yet?

The car suddenly conked out
In a sulky puff of steam and
Mum shooed us away, "Go 'n' play
in the farmer's field ... over there."

We ran and ran … as only kids can,
Until the field stole our breath and
Flung us ... on our backs, gasping
Like mad for air ... and we lay there ...

Staring at the threadbare clouds,
Higher than high … in the jigsaw sky,
And forgot all about the tinfoil sea,
On that day ... we were nearly there.

The Boy On Our Bus

If I just owned those gorgeous shoes:
Those crimson criss-cross espadrilles ...
He'd notice me!

The boy on our bus:
The one with long hair,
Who sits at the back ...
I try not to stare!

If I grew my hair and wore it loose,
Padded my bra for a bit of a boost ...
He might glance over!

The boy on our bus:
The one with a tan,
Who sits at the back ...
I need a plan!

If I gave up eating anything fried,
Lost an inch off each of my thighs ...
He'd be bound to look then!

The boy on our bus:
The one with nice jeans,
Who sits at the back ...
Oh look my way please!

Of course,
I was ever-so shy ...
If he'd looked my way,
I'd probably have died.

Loose Bird

Back in the day ... in my 20s,
I was temping at 3M ... when
Come home-time, I needed a push
To get my old Mini started again!

Chorus:
Keep your revs up, no matter what you do,
Mightn't be anyone to bump-start you!

Off I went and I have to say:
My nerves were all of a jangle!
I hadn't long passed my driving test,
And the stress was hard to handle!

Chorus

It was gorgeous sunny weather,
As I headed out of town ...
I was enjoying the breeze ... my
car-windows rolled right down.

Chorus

I drove over a small humpback bridge,
And got one helluva of a shock:
My windscreen was obscured by a
swathe of sparrows, flying in a flock!

Chorus

Somehow I managed to keep driving,
In a split-second the sparrows had gone.
I was, truth be told, quite shaken ...
A bit of a close call ... that one!

Chorus

But it turned out, one of the sparrows
Hadn't flown away after all!
He was there in my rear view mirror,
Damn! ... I slowed right down to a crawl!

Chorus

He was fluttering on the back seat,
It'd be fine if he just stayed there,
But then he started hopping around:
It was becoming a right nightmare!

Chorus

The sparrow landed in the footwell,
And that gave me pause for thought!
I pulled up ... but kept the car running,
At this stage, it was all very fraught!

Chorus

I only had 2 doors on my old Mini,
So I flung them both open-wide!
And got out to apologise:
"Sorry ... there's a loose bird inside!"

Chorus

The sparrow had seized his moment
And escaped to look for his friends!
The bloke behind looked disappointed ...
And that's where this anecdote ends!

Except to say, "Girls, in Your Twenties,
Don't worry! No matter what you do,
There'll always be blokes aplenty,
More than happy to bump-start you!"

Fast Forward A Few Years

Heavily pregnant with my second child,
And living in a flat in France,
I was slobbing about in an old T-shirt,
And my husband's pyjama pants ...

When I went to answer the door to the
Caretaker of our apartment block,
Who had arrived unexpectedly
With a loud and purposeful knock.

I've no clue what he was after,
My school French was quite poor
But he seemed happy enough to
Just hover there at my front door.

In the end ... I had to wind things up,
Stopped just short of giving him a push,
Only noticed, after I shut the door, that
Sprouting from those PJs was ... my bush.

The Weather Forecast

Whatever lovely Schafernaker says,
It won't make much difference to me,
I went into a tropical heatwave
During the decade .... after 2003.

"Miss, what's the matter with your face?
Why are you soaking wet?"
"It's a funny time of life Dylan,
I doubt your mum's got there yet!"

One minute I'm freezing 'n' the next:
Crossing the Sahara with no camel,
Flipping heck ... this is embarrassing!
"Has anyone got a spare flannel?"

As you boys reach for your Harleys,
Us girls are getting good at whipping:
Cardigans on and cardigans off ...
No pole-dancing ... just stripping!

A Granddaughter

Wow!
How she smoothed
Out the wrinkles,
Added some crinkles to put
a smile on Grandpa's face.

And as he raced
ahead into the night,
Nan caught sight of
his beaming lights,
Hitched a lift to
brush off old rifts,
Risk one more spin
'round the ring road,
One more jaunt
down Harmony Lane ...
Hallelujah ... it's
'Happy Hour' again ...

Wow! Grandpa's
amazing saving grace,
How she lit up
the laugh lines on
his handsome face!

I'm A Widow ...

and as well as the loss, it seems that
God is the most unsympathetic boss!

No manager ever called me in for a chat,
Saying "You look sad ... we can help
with that ...
We're getting rid of your colleague Fred,
Putting you in charge of plumbing instead!

Also keep an eye on the ridge tiles, Love,
You don't want water coming in from above!
If taps start to dance with a rhythmic drip,
Or paintwork to peel with pockmarked chips,

That's all part of your job description now!
What do you mean ... you don't know how?
And don't forget to clean out the gutters,
Was that a rude word that you muttered?

If you really can't cope with this simple stuff,
You'll have to pay ... but it'll be quite tough,
To avoid being taken for an expensive ride ...
"Flipping heck ... why did he have to go and die?"

Wellies

February '22 was wild,
Storm Dudley came howling through,
Uprooting my huge leylandii,
And Number Four's conifers too.

It was insurance pandemonium ...
No tree surgeons for love nor money,
But although it was muddy underfoot,
The next day was bright and sunny.

Number Four rang to ask me over
for a biscuit and a cup of tea,
To discuss what to do about
Our respective fallen trees.

So I chucked on my wellies and
departed post-haste for hers ... to
Learn she'd found some tree-blokes
Who'd agreed ... to head over there.

I'd drunk my tea 'n' put my wellies back on,
By the time the two blokes arrived,
And we asked if they could pop down to
Me ... afterwards ... if they had the time.

Then something ... rather unexpected ...
"You're ... wearing ... boots ..." the first
bloke leered,
"They're just my wellies, "I answered,
Sensing ... something a little bit weird.

The second bloke must've felt compelled,
To utter the following ... explanation:
"He's got a real ... thing ... about ... boots",
Like it was a sort of recommendation.

But ... me being me ... I made it worse ...
I waffled on about muddy weather,
And added, "They're just Dunlop wellies,
Not black ... thigh high ... laced-up...leather!"

Welly-Fetish-Bloke's expression
was priceless ...
His eyes stood right out on stalks,
As I shuffled to Number Four's gate,
Attempting a calm-unflustered walk.

But ... off I took... at a high speed run ...
 As soon as I was out of view ...
 It's quite hard to run in wellies,
Wellies are a ... liability ... let me tell you!

Meantime my thoughts were racing,
And it's amazing just how speedy ...
Is the whirring of a panicked-mind ...
Under pressure ... when it needs to be.

I went to borrow Next-door's-Husband ...
She didn't mind ... I looked a right mess,
Poor man ... he's NOT into wellies ...
... And he was visibly ... under duress.

Needless to say boots weren't mentioned,
When the tree-chaps came to quote ,
And ... after 'careful consideration',
I ... just didn't go with those blokes.

18 months on ..

I think Next-Door's Husband is still
Dubious ... gives me some funny looks,
Probably thinks it was all in my head ...
Or I've read too many racy books.

But what on earth ... was I thinking ...
I must have been raving mad ...!
A practical bloke with the hots for me:
A bonkers poet ... and welly-clad!

When

... the sympathy cards stop coming
and the blooming flowers fade.

When I've made the calls and filled
the forms, what of the plans we made?

I don't think I'll buy that caravan ...
I'd cause havoc if I tried towing.

'One-woman-went-to-mow' sounds
wrong but grass just keeps on growing!

I miss you coming home, dumping
your laptop bag ... on the chair.

Now ... I'd just love to see you ... go
ahead ... chuck your bag ... anywhere.

Part 3:

Pure Daftness

New School Shoes

Once a year at the end of August,
Mums buy the new shoes for school,
Jed's feet are practically square so
They had to be measured, as a rule.

2009 : the year Jed turned eleven,
The shoe shop was totally packed
With mums and kids in the 4 to
7 age-bracket ... hard to be exact,

The assistant measured Jed's feet and
Loudly announced to my silent swearing,
"Your son is measuring a very wide six,
But that's only size 4 that he's wearing."

Never in my life ... have I encountered
such a collective-disapproval-stare,
It brought out my very worst side and
So ... feigning an irresponsible air ...

I came back with the following reply,
"It's ok ... I tucked his toes under ...
You know ... ancient Chinese-style."
A sudden hush ... louder than thunder

And a roomful of righteous mothers,
All fiercely glaring in my direction ...
Wondering ... whether or not to get
On their phones to Child-Protection.

Just in case there are those among
You ... who are feeling slightly shocked,
Don't worry ... Jed is 25 now and
He'd spent that whole summer in Crocs.

The Eyelash Tint

My daughter wanted a career change,
Took a short beautician's course,
Painted all of our nails and
Then ... came her tour de force ...

She said she'd tint my eyelashes,
If I picked up a DIY kit,
So I popped out to get one,
Slightly worried ... I admit.

She did it in her lunchtime,
And it was all a bit of a rush,
But she was doing it for free,
So I didn't want to make a fuss.

Except to comment that
The under-eye pads ... felt stiff,
And God ... when she peeled them off,
They were more like waxing strips.

Afterwards when I read the box,
I was ... not entirely surprised
She'd used a free sample of tit tape ...
On my ... delicate under eyes.

There Was Once

... an enormous walrus,
Named after Norse god: Thor!
He sought refuge on our coastline,
Not seen one like him before!

All the way up to Scarborough,
Folks flocked in droves to stare,
But due to health 'n' safety,
It was a stand-well-back affair ...

Nearly a ton of walrus with
Protruding dental structure!
An inch too close to his tusks,
Could cause a helluva puncture!

Scarborough cancelled the fireworks:
No bangs on New Year's Eve ... then
With a flagrant waggle of his flippers,
Thor ... promptly ... took his leave!

Super Lucky

Went and did my Sainsbury's shop earlier,
First time for ages ... I'd worn jeans,
Congratulated myself on getting better
at using their self-check-out machines.

And remembering ... I need the receipt
To be released ... without delay,
I actually felt a little bit smug about
Getting my act together today.

Until ... as I was loading the boot,
And trying not to break the eggs,
A random pair of knickers showed up ...
Fell out of one of my trouser-legs.

If that had happened in the shop,
It would not have been the best,
So next time ... I put on jeans,
I'll be carrying out ... a knicker-test.

I Went Out Out ...

And didn't get hung over but
Got a bit of a crick in my neck,
I chose the wrong seat on the
train ... my own fault ... blooming heck!

Forgot the "look before you leap" advice,
Jumped in ... opposite a man-spreader ...
Trying to cool down... not trying to entice.

And to be fair ... it was a very warm night,
But ... not only were his legs akimbo,
His short shorts were ... ever-so tight.

He was that buff rugby-build kind of fit,
Probably thought I'd sat opposite
him on purpose ... to ogle at his bits.

Oh no ... should I get up and move?
Or ride it out ... like I was the ...
macho one with something to prove?

So awkward but I couldn't back down,
Got the wonky neck from "averting
my gaze" ... all the way into town.

Much Maligned Dandelions ...

Scourge of green-lawn fanatics,
But ... how fantastic ... are
Those swaying meadows
... Of teetering stilettos!
Flamboyant blooms with
Bold-as-brass plumes!
Floozies of flirtatious antics,
Brazen, ooh la la ...
Sounds ever-so romantic,
But dandelions are blasé,
Do their thing ... their own way ...
No swiping right ... "Gosh he looks fit!"
Their seeds ... maternal identikits!

Nevertheless
Here come the bees!
All abuzz with expertise!
Great hairy legs there,
Wow what a derrière!
Such warm fuzzy passion,
Haut-couture velvet fashion!
Looking for action:
For sweet satisfaction!

And dandelions do provide
Nectar starter ... pollen side ...
Sticky toffee pud for bees ...
"Tuck right in, if you please!"
Canoodling galore on
The bumble-bee chase,
But it's girl-power magic
That really takes place.

Flowers swiftly fray to frills,
Fields of ballet-tutu thrills
Breathless ...
For that high-flying dance,
The flimsy chiffon chance,
To pirouette on the breeze ...
A springtime feast for our bees.

Part 4:

Stuff to Think About

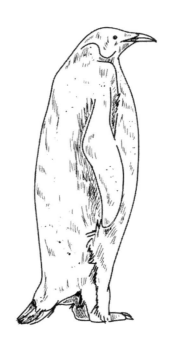

Who Knows ...

Move over C3PO,
Realistic humanoids are on their way,
With tiny micro-expressions to
Nuance every word they say ...

Could be an amazing breakthrough
For the lonely house-bound elderly ...
Who knows ... some of us ... just
Might ... get treated ... tenderly!

Invasive Species

There's a new army of ants on the move,
And entomologists don't approve,
But why on Earth should us lot care?
Red fire ants ... aren't really our affair.
I mean ... they're not in the UK yet,
Nowhere near an imminent threat,
They're miles away on Italian shores,
Mustering powerful super-hordes
Of colonies with multiple queens,
Invaders who'd like to treat us mean:

Wreak havoc on our insects and crops,
Rack up prices in local shops,
Take up residence in the family car,
And as if, all that's ... not a step too far,
Infest the innards of our high tech stuff ...
They really know how to cut up rough.

But what if it's us?
If we're the threat ... to life ... light years away?
And they're desperate to keep us ... at bay?
Imagine the panic ...and clamour of bells...
Now we're set ... to muck up the moon ...
as well.

Those Guys

Penguins are so cute and fluffy,
It's hard to hear of their demise,
But who on Earth gives a damn
About those Phytoplankton Guys.

The name is somewhat off-putting,
It's ...all Greek to me,
Google says "plant wanderers" ...
Or ... drifters of the sea.

But they're busy absorbing CO_2,
And putting oxygen into our air,
Getting on with it ... so quietly
We hardly know they're there.

No need whatsoever ... to worry,
Those Guys will keep on keeping on,
Unless the ocean gets too warm,
Then ... just like that ... gone ...

The Emergency-Alert

At 3pm on Sunday, came the siren:
The government's brand new alert,
Piercingly-loud and shocking ...
My labrador's ears were hurt!

Good to know they're planning
For the day Putin sends his nukes,
We know he's got it in him ...
Just look how low he stoops!

But some folks didn't get the call,
Their mobiles failed to ring,
Big Brother had forgotten them,
Not so much as a muted ping!

They're probably the lucky ones,
A nuke's one of our biggest dreads,
And that kind of early-warning
Would totally wreck our heads!

Now us "chosen ones" are waiting
For Rishi to issue us with our lead ...
No 2 metre rule or handwashing
Will halt ... nuclear radiation spread!

Part 5:

Me, Myself & I

Mr Darcy

You can keep your Chippendales,
They just don't do it for me!
It's been all about Mr Darcy,
Since nineteen-seventy-three!

Later came the TV series,
With Colin Firth as the star:
Stripped to the waist for a swim,
He whipped up a right hoo-ha!

But my favourite actor to
Be cast in the famous part,
Is Matthew MacFadyen:
He stole my lascivious heart!

But now it's all over and my
fantasies have been dashed!
He'll forever be John Stonehouse...
Hope ITV paid him lots of cash!

Dress Sense

My daughter is horrified
By most of the clothes I wear
She says I need Gok Wan's help ...
But I think he's gone off air!

My son says I'm 'rainbow-fied',
Throw multiple colours at it,
But bold colours make me happy,
... I'm simply a creature of habit.

Sometimes ... I leave home,
Thinking that I look great,
Spot myself in a shop window,
And realise ... my mistake.

Think what I need to do is
... Actually look in the mirror,
Or just tell the pair of them
To stop trying to interfere!

Thrill Seeker

Got to be early at boot sales,
Few worms ... many hungry birds,
One man's trash ... your treasure ...
Amid the troves of trivial and absurd.

Me ... I'm much less committed,
Yet ... I share the same passion,
Love ... rifling through charity-
shop-rails of outmoded fashions.

Am I in search of a new outfit?
Or seeking that buzzing sensation?
The high of a designer jacket for
Fifteen quid ... that's retail-elation.

Flipping Heck

I open my mouth,
And words ... just spew out ...
My brain is not involved,
Power has been devolved.

But when speech clicks off,
How my mind does scoff!
That's when it's in its prime,
Can take the proper time ...

To think about the things I've said,
What I meant to say instead,
'n' how to possibly put it right,
Going to be ... one of those nights.

Daring Deeds

My daughter in law went skydiving
'n' chucked herself out of a plane,
But I get vertigo just looking upwards
at things like skyscrapers 'n' cranes!

I did once go kayaking with Karin:
A few miles along the River Wye,
And there was a rather-angry swan,
Who got very cross at us passing by.

And Liz and I were nearly drowned
on a day trip to Weston-Super-Mare,
But that was accidental ... the tide
goes out a shocking-long-way there!

As a rule, these kind of hazardous
things don't really float my boat ...
My idea of daring is to walk round
Waitrose with my PJs under my coat!

It's A Mystery

Everything in our world is made of Matter:
Everything that matters to you and me ...

Why wasn't it cancelled out by Antimatter?
Why did either triumph? ... It's a mystery!

Light should have been all that was left
in the wake of that famous big bang,

But after billions of years ... there was a
universe ... 'n' eventually there was ... man.

Our scientists are on the case ... they're
Saying Antimatter does feels Gravity's pull,

But does it move at the exact-same speed?

And why is MY grey matter cotton wool?

END

Printed in Great Britain
by Amazon

34029686R00031